Elisabeth Du Puy

The dragon yoke

Elisabeth Du Puy

The dragon yoke

ISBN/EAN: 9783337273897

Printed in Europe, USA, Canada, Australia, Japan

Cover: Foto ©Andreas Hilbeck / pixelio.de

More available books at **www.hansebooks.com**

TO

SIR PHILIP SIDNEY.

CONTENTS.

CONTENTS.

THE DRAGON YOKE.

SONNETS.

THE DESERTED HOUSE.

DARK is thy dwelling; thro' the silent night
   The shadow o'er its desolate threshold swings,
   And on the icy eaves the low moon flings
The sudden fire of its re-risen light,
Upon the frosty windows glancing white,
   And to the pallor of the peaked roof clings;
   In the bare boughs the wind like a bugle rings
And on the glittering drifts wreaks its despite :

Alas, my darling, alas, my roving one,
   That wandereth far away from love and me,
When will the skies bring back a warmer sun
   And summer winds, whispering sweet thoughts to
      thee,
Woo thee again to thine enchanted West
   And to the refuge of this soft fond breast ?

HER WHITE SHAPE 'GAINST THE AMETHYST.

NOT, not alone in old and fabled fanes,
　　Where kings are crowned and mailèd knights repose
　　(In smooth marble commemorate, as on those
Pale monoliths which watch the Persian plains),
But also in the city's peopled mains
　　Dwelleth that spirit mystical : where throws
　　The moon her aureole, and silvery shows
Her white shape 'gainst the amethyst campagne;
And where aspiring boughs, Oh, pale and fair,
　　Roof the still way with canopy of laves,
Where the thin wavering shadow ofttimes falls,
　　There dwelleth the Divine : one passing there
In seeming treads, entranced, Olympian halls.

MERCURY THE SPARKLER.

QUICK as the shadows fall, with wingèd flight
　　He drives his milky flocks to fields afar,
　　And long before the Wain, on noiseless bar
Thro' half its arc has turned, along the height
Has pastured them; 'tis he that steals the light
　　From misty mead and hill, and every star,
　　And horned Astarte in her golden car,
Lures down the blue abysm toward the night.

Fair Herald of the wingèd cap and feet,
　　Thou of each shy and nimble thought the god,
Who art the source of fancies light and fleet.

Come thou and touch the dull and earthy clod
With thy caduceus, and my soul inspire
With thy resistless, ever-soaring fire !

HOPE'S RETURN.

BLACK was the night, and ever in my dream
   A skeleton sat grimly by my bed;
    Without, the air was peopled with the dead,
The wind's voice was in semblance like the scream
Which echoes o'er Cocytus' pallid stream;
   And evermore the phantom at my head
    Smiled ghastly on me; methought also he fed
Upon my heart; most keen his fang did seem:
But as beset and tortured thus I lay,
   It seemed as tho' the fearful clouds were rent,
And lo ! a rainbow, stretched from heaven to me;
   Sweet harps and cymbals then began to play,
Whereat an angel his white pinions bent
   Adown the blue, and kissed me joyously.

THE MOONLIT AVENUE.

THIS is the portico of that great fane
   Which is the temple where my muse doth dwell
    What time she deigns to bless me with the spell
Of her mysterious power; the shining plane
Lies there, and there my weary spirit fain,
   Down-sinking in the light as in a well,
    Would linger lulled forever by the swell
Of winds that voice our human joy and pain:

Yon columned trees are made for sculptured walls,
　The leafless boughs for indented roof;
Sad music murmurs thro' these broken halls
　And here the moonlight weaves its shining woof,
And shapes of leaf and pendant spray it throws
To flutter in each idle wind that blows.

THE GARDEN THEATRE.

A ROSE, a garden and a handsome face,
　Sweet Juliet's hour and Romeo near by,
　The moon a silvery beacon flaming high,
And silvery echoes sounding in its trace;
Where thick and dim the green boughs interlace,
　Wherewith soft languishment the breezes sigh
　And crystal stars burn in a sapphire sky,
And forms of bright similitude and grace
　Move in the pageantry of rainbow hues,
Like tulips dancing in a drowsy wind:
　And then anon they sang of youth and love,
　(Girl-dancers all, in fluttering reds and blues):
Oh Love, so fell thine arrows keen and kind,
　Like meteors flashing from the blue above.

THE OZARKS.

STILL deck thy brows with coronals of light,
　The hills I love, and woo the gilded blaze
　From hazel brakes and fields of tasseled maize,
From sunflowers a-tremble with the flight

Of bobolinks that flee the autumn blight,
From purple thistle by the tangled ways
Woo thitherward wild sweets and let the rays
Of tawny clouds clothe thee in raiment bright:

So glorified the sun has stooped to thee,
Laid to thine amethyst a kiss of fire;
Yet while about thee sweeps the tuneful choir
Of birds and breezes, darkly at thy knee
The river beats, dim as the stream of gloom
O'er which sad souls are ferried to their doom.

GREEN APRIL-TIDE.

Now is the time leaves put forth tender green,
And our chill streets renew former delight,
Flaunting fresh glories on the charmèd sight;
The frogs' love-songs arise from rainpools clean,
And vistas show dreamlike thro' misty sheen:
This hour the sun, a giant in his might,
Drops huge and red away, and, lo, 'tis night,
With starry sentinels guarding the scene:
Ah, with what homesick longing now I think
How the hills are white with drift of dog-wood bloom,
How in the grass frail little wind-flowers dance,
How the robins sing in the peach-trees' spires of pink:
At nightfall apple boughs make sweet the gloom,—
Oh, might I breathe again that fine fragrance !

THE HARBOR.

Unto the stormless shelter of that bay,
Where idly round the green and sedgy shore
Murmuring wave to wavelet ever more

Makes dreamy music thro' the sunlit day,
And fluttering in the gold or misty ray
   White-winged sea-gulls do lightly wheel and soar
   And every snowy sail, the seas far o'er,
Against a dim blue summit courts the gale;

Turns he with wistful gaze; the voyage done,
   Old griefs will be forgot, and dreamfully
His eyes survey the tranquil setting sun.
   Tho' now about him breaks the raging sea,
His heart foreknows the danger will be past
And into harbor he will float at last.

THE SPIRIT'S CRY.

WHEN saffron morning, breaking o'er the realms of gloom
   Recalls the wandering soul again to weary life,
     I, leaving those dim scenes with care and tumult rife,
To woo the Beautiful thro' vales where still groves loom,
Find death's insignia first, upon the hoary tomb;
   Now ceased from sorrow and from Fate's unkindly
     strife,
   They lie forgot, nor call to arms, nor warning fife,
Nor dawn's red beam may wake them from their dream-
     less sleep:

Along the Orient where burns the violet,
   Still sheds the Day-star far abroad his golden fire—
   The namesake fair of him whom God in righteous
     ire
Cast o'er the heavenly City's glittering parapet;
   Oh Lucifer, thou star of morn-illumined skies,
   How, like to thee, have I lamented Paradise!

THE RED RISING MOON.

THERE was none to gainsay or oppose, and therefore we
    went
    Thro' the shadow encolumned aisles, where poplar
       trees
    Made midnight, and through their spiry tops the
       breeze
With breath of enchantment sang, and the stars, for-
    spent
In their purple ascensions, no silvery glamourings lent,
    But dusk, deep dusk, of the hour from cock-crowing
       one,
    Hung there, and crickets creaked in the grasses dun,—
There was none to gainsay and we wandered hither con-
    tent.

Sweet, and thrice-sweet, the thoughts and musical dreams
    That are wrought by the magic of a rising mid-sum-
       mer moon,
    Thrice-sweet, and blended with memories tender and
       sad:
    Ah, tears! But, soft you,—the red moon is up, and
       her beams
Bar the pathway mysterious: now o'er the ruddy pon-
    toon
    Pass, passionate pilgrims — the mid-summer moon
    makes mad.

THE DESOLATE HEART. '

IF thou, mine angel, couldst return to me
Out of thy blest and changeless peace on high,
This troubled heart whose unsolaced distress
So long hath vexed the nights of loneliness,
Mourned old bereavement with new constancy,
And given each hour the largess of a sigh,
No more the fool of fancies idly dreamed,
From sorrow's servitude should be redeemed:
And can it be that even all the bliss
In which thy golden throne is surely set
Hath made thy loyal heart, beloved, forget
The pain, the grief, the agony of this ?
Is it not rather that with yearning eyes
Thou lookst upon me from yon soft blue skies?

SONGS.

Whenever the moon is white like this,
I dream of a time of foregone bliss,—
    All past and done,
    With yesterday's sun !
The moon shines golden against the leaf,—
The sight of its shadow brings me grief:
    All past and fled,
    Sealed up and dead !
The moon, like a shield in the azure sky,
Minds me of summers long gone by,—
    All past and dead,
    And vanished !

HESPER.

Go not, sweet star, so soon,
    For scarce has paled the violet
    Along the east, nor yet
Has risen o'er the hills the silver sickled moon;
    Sweet one, go not so soon!

Dusk veils the window, sweet,
    But 'neath the lilied breast
    The wistful heart, in wild unrest,
Still throbs with passionate beat.

Tho' after thee should rise,
    Oh love, a myriad stars to fret
    The circling blue, Oh yet,
Rayless would seem the night and dark the boundless
    skies,
    Shorn of the splendor of thine eyes!

MONBARS.

AFTER SEEING MR. MANTELL IN THE PLAY—1889.

As I went thro' the rosy glen,
    (Oh love, so fine and fair)
I felt the salt wind from the sea
Blow tense against my breast and knee
    And coldly beat on cheeks and hair;
My blood rushed quick, as fired with wine,
    (Dear love, so fair and fine.)

As I went down the sandy beach,
    (Ah love, far o'er the sea)
I saw the pale ships on the wave
Come sailing from the blue concave;
    And while I gazed the heart in me
Was thrilled with ecstasy and fear,
    (Dear love, in harbor near).

As I went thro' the sea-ward glen,
    The waves sang, " Come," Monbars;
Between the white spray and the moon
I felt me clasped in arms eftsoon;
    Sweet wooed the nightingales afar;
Lo, as his mouth in rapture kissed,
    The stars swooned o'er us, thro' the mist.

FROM THE SAND-HILLS AND THE SEA.

HAVE you a pipe, have you a flute?
   I would you made melody—I am sad:
The nightingales all were long since mute,
    (The song of the nightingale never was glad
    And they say thát moonlight makes men mad)
Tho' surely sorrow has maddened me,
Sorrow for loss of joys we had,
   By the yellow sand-hills and the sea.

Now, a happy vision last night was mine,
   As I lay sleeping on my soft bed;
I dreamt of the ships and the sunny brine,
    I dreamt of my dear love—long since dead;
    A darksome water went over her head,
But I think of her oftenest, walking with me,
   Whenever the moon cleaves a pathway red
Thro' the yellow sand-hills and the sea.

Oh, let it be pipe or ivory flute,
   How glad soever the measure ring,
And, tho' the nightingales be not mute,
    I wot of that the waves will sing;
    I wot how her feet went wandering
Far from the ways of love and me,
   From the flowing tide and the wavering wing,
Far from the sand-hills and the sea

L'ENVOY.

Whenever the moon sets red in the west,
Still does the picture return to me,—
   The shadowy beach and the boats at rest,
The light on the sand-hills and the sea.

THE CUCKOO'S CALL.

Now dost thou hear the cuckoo call,
  Below the breeze-blown daffodils ?
  The bursting of the bubbling rills
And passing of the icy pall
  He celebrates in chorals clear,
  Here in the spring-tide of the year.
Betwixt the yellow and the green,

  The cuckoo calls ; O sweet, O sweet,
  The white-thorn blooms above the wheat ;
The unruffled lakelet's crystal sheen
  Lies open to the azure sphere,
  Bright in the spring-tide of the year.

But not for me young April's mirth :
  Dost thou remember how, one day,
  Thou, perjured one, didst turn away ?
Across the heavens and the earth,
  Ah, "False" is written, as a scroll
  That grimmest demon-hands unroll.

THE UNHEEDING GODS.—TRICOLET.

You may weep, indeed, if you please,
  And make the night windy with sighs,—
There's no such cure for disease :
You may weep indeed if you please,
And implore on your bended knees
  The burnished, unheeding skies ;
You may weep indeed if you please,—
  But the gods your tears despise :

THE WONDER WORLD.

I DREAMT a silver star was set,
A jewel in the sapphire sky ;
Upon the hill-tops, dusk and high,
The fir-trees and the cedars met
In lines of mosque and minaret
Against the lucid gleaming gold ;
And in the valley, deep in shade,
The ring-dove soft complaining made,
And ivory flutes sweet love-notes told.
Beneath the purpling parapet.

I dreamt the groves did grow so sweet
In that enchanted land of love ;
The milk-white blossoms bent above
The silent waters' crystal sheet ;
The blue air throbbed with bliss complete,
And in the still, green solitudes
The light was like a Summer moon
Across the yellow fields in June,
And nightingales their clear preludes
Sang in the grasses at our feet.

I dreamt a palace great and fair,
Whose towers were like the crystal, kissed
By dawning suns, rose thro' the mist,
With bastions sculptured on the air,
With arch and carven column rare:
And, gleaming on the dusk afar,

Its marble façades, polished white
As snow-peaks in a frosty light ;
And mild, lucernal, as a star,
Each window's amethystine glare.

Soft as the night hours slid away
I saw green meadows turn to gold ;
By silvery brooks the shepherd's fold
Guarded his snowy lambs when Day
Withdrew her irridescent ray,
And down the violet-scented path
Came one, a prince of high degree ;
The same is lord of love and me ;
His look all kind persuasion hath
And he in Arcady holds sway.

L'ENVOY.

This is the spirit's bright estate,
And this that sweetheart, bard and king
Of whose dear love, betimes and late,
My soul doth daily strive to sing ;
This, ere the late moon's light was spent,
Was the sweet vision that I dreamt.

REMEMBER ME.

WHEN the sweet end hath all thy fond hopes crowned,
And mirth and song and flowers decked thee around,
    Remember me, remember me !
Who oft in darkest hours took thought for thee,
    Remember me !

To those dear years, the unforgotten years,
Wherein we shared our happiness and tears,
   Let some kind thought, fond thought return;
Shut not thy love within a tomb so stern,
   Let some kind thought return.

Thou wast not wont to be so churlish cold,
Such hard proud looks were not thy looks of old ;
   Alas, Untrue, Untrue!
Wilt thou let old friends be displaced by new ?
   Forsworn, Untrue!

PROSERPINE.

THERE is a voice calls in the reeds,—
   Do not delay, do not delay,
   Young Proserpine passes this way,—
   Do not delay, do not delay!
So sings the soft voice in the reeds,
So whispers in the lush green water-weeds.

She has a gilt veil to her head,
   Fair Proserpine, the dainty queen;
   Her garments are of rustling green,
   Her short mantle of fleecy sheen;
About her all the stars are spread,
And mystic suns on her their aureoles shed.

Behold, for her in the yellow fields
   The speckled partridge whistles clear,
   And lorn frogs in the shallow weir
   Are croaking far and croaking near;
And when the moon lifts high her shield
The oaten pipe does tender music yield.

Great scarlet poppies now she strews
  And makes the low plain red with them;
  She gathers many a lily stem,
  For her white brows a diadem;
Nor heed she that beyond the yews
The chariot horses strain their thews.

WHEN ROSES SCATTERED LIE.

HAST thou forgot those golden days,
Hast thou forgot those woodland ways,
  The flowers that blossomed red and white,
  The blue that arched the heavenly height,
The birds that carolled high and clear,
Hast thou forgot, hast thou forgot, my dear ?

Hast thou forgot those shadowy walks,
Hast thou forgot our murmured talks,
  The moon that silvery shone o'er head,
  What time the day evanishéd ?
The sweet caress, the tender kiss,
Hast thou forgot, oh love, all this ?

Hast thou forgot, hast thou forgot,
Is thine a heart that alters not ?
  Thy speech is cold, and colder still
  Thine eyes, that smite me with their chill,
And I would know, beloved one,
If thou art changed with Summer's sun.

ALAS, ALAS !

THAT ever day should dawn so black,
  Alas, alas, my love,
We cannot call the sunshine back,
  Or bring the blue above;

The rain falls cold, the red leaves fly,
The pale blooms on the trellis die.
Winds pipe shrill and branches sigh,
Bright summer days have all gone by,
  Alas, my love!

That ever the world was made so wide,
  Alas, alas, my sweet !
We cannot bridge the sea's salt tide,
  Or make the two ways meet;
The ships sail east, the ships sail west,
They seek far empires in their quest,
They bear much treasure, all unguessed
They take from us that we love best,
  Alas, my sweet!

That ever words such shape should take,
  Alas, alas my dear!.
How shall I by rude symbols make
  My tender feelings clear ?
Thou hast of me sov'reign control
Thou art of life and hope the whole,
Then why should seas between us roll,
  Alas, my dear!

I ENVY THE MEN.—TRIOLET.

I envy the men :
  " What ? " do you wonder ?
'Tis not their beards, then,
That I envy the men,
But their right to say, when
  Provocation they're under,
I envy the men,—
  Oh, you go to thunder.

.

GOLD HAIR.

Gold Hair, Gold Hair, thou hast my soul undone;
For of thy shining gold a web hast spun,
Hast caught me fast within the silken snare,
Hast strangled me with silken, shining hair.

Thy roseleaf laughing lips, so sweet to kiss,
They maddened me, they made me drunk with bliss;
Not all the wine to empurple all the seas
Might intoxicate men's senses, love, as these!

Oh, have I not beneath this very moon
Tasted such joys as made my senses swoon?
How oft beneath these star-pulsating skies,
I've drowned me in the splendor of thine eyes!

Gold Hair, and dusky eyes, wilt thou atone
For that dark deed I did—for thee alone?
At midnight, when the wolf barked on the hill,
At midnight, when the world was tranced and still,

Barefoot I stole upon him while he slept;
The moon, an angel, guard beside him kept;
The moon's white fingers, cross his bare throat lay;
I made her lustre show me how to slay.

Oh, dark eyes amorous, hast wept for him
Until thy splendor is eclipsed and dim?
Alas, to see thy hair's gold glory spread
Above his beauty, when I left him dead!

I could have killed thee when thy satin gown
Was rent to staunch his dark blood trickling down:
Hush !   Am I mad, or dreaming that thy blood
Leaped up and stained me with its purple flood ?

O God! mad, mad am I, chained in this cell
Damned, doomed forever with the fiends to dwell!
And thou hast done it, lily-limbed and fair,
Hast dragged to hell with strands of golden hair!

Before that thou wast false, in old sweet hours,
Dwelling with me mid roses and white flowers,
Oft have I held thee so, close to me pressed—
Sweeter than roses, pale and soft of breast.

Like wine the memory yet inflames my veins,
As at a moon the sweet flood flows and wanes,
Till sometimes hell and torture are forgot
And naught of anything but love I wot.

Gold Hair, is it thus and but in such wise
The damned soul suffers, and but in this guise
That demons come, with faces fond and fair
Glancing from under veils of gilded hair ?

LILY AND ROSES.—TRICOLET.

FROM THE GARDEN SCENE IN " DEN-MY-CHREE."

Oh, turn thy face toward me, sweet,
    On thy cheeks bloom the lily and rose;
Thy lilies the moonbeams do greet,
Oh turn thy face toward me, sweet,
That thine eyes my fond eyes may meet,
    On thy roses the firelight glows:
Oh, turn thy face toward me, sweet,
    On thy cheeks bloom the lily and rose.

A LOVER WILD AND PALE.

AND now, when earthly lovers flee,
By dawn, by dusk, who wooeth me ?
    The way o'er which the moonbeams lie,
    Or where the star opens wide its eye,
Or where the sunset shineth red
Upon yon oak-crowned mountain's head,
    The way whence faithless lovers flee
    Who cometh here awooing me ?

Pale is his face, so sweetly pale,
With wandering locks that make a veil
    Before his wild and tender een;
    His voice breathes as a harp atween
The passionate winds that wildly blow
Thro' groves where bristly pine-trees grow;
    He is a poet, sweetly pale
    Behind his love-locks' golden veil.

And when he woos, his speech doth tell
Of homes where all the voiceless dwell—
    The homes where none ere breathes a word,
    Where neither harp nor song is heard,
But all in peace they lie, and keep
Close-wrapped the veil of trancèd sleep;
    For never sound may break the spell
    Of those that with the dead do dwell.

Haply some night, o'er-awed and mute,
I'll yield me to Death's gentle suit,
    And hand-in-hand, as with a friend,
    Into the grave will I descend;
No more in weariness and pain,
No more lamenting blight and rain,
    Close-clasped unto my bridegroom's breast,
    I shall take long and pleasant rest.

ENDYMION'S LOVE SONG.

Whose feet came over my mountains
    Between sun setting and morn ?
She passed along by the fountains,
    And faint was her silver horn.

Now Apollo his steeds down the blue steeps
    Drives fast, and the serpentine
Pale line of the myrmidon mists creeps
    O'er meadows and copses green :

Now stars are faint in the golden
    Deep glow of the darkening skies,
Oh, fly with the stars thro' the olden
    Dim path that the swallow flies !

Silene, who fleeth the bright day,
    How green is our Latmian hill !
Now winds thro' the groves breathe a soft lay,
    And the cavern is dim and still :

Sweet dreams o'er my eye-lids hover,—
    Be thou to me more than a dream ;
Oh, break thro' the slumberous cover,
    Come with thy silverly gleam.

Lo, warm on my lips thy kisses,
   And soft as Æolian gales,
When the asphodel, reviving old blisses.
   Bursts billow-like o'er the vales.

IN THE PARK.

I saw thy banks, sweet river, clothed with green ;
   The golden leaves bent to thy dazzling blue,
   And there the crested jay-bird's rivalling hue
Was briefly mirrored in thy placid sheen.

The weeping-willow drooped its pendant spray,
   The sumach spread its mottled scarlet cloak,
   And gay leaves fallen from the towering oak,
Along the slopes and in the hollows lay.

A pungent perfume chilly breezes bore,
   The thistle shook abroad its flossy hair ;
   The acorn and the hickory-nut were there,
To drive grim famine from the squirrel's door.

The fountain, like a noiseless ghost, stood white
   Against the sunny background of the sky ;
   Far on the blue horizon could descry
The silhouettes of bare trees on the height.

The cawing of the solemn-coated crow
   Dropped listless down the depths of purple haze ;
   A touch of frost upon the crimson ways
Proclaimed the coming of a conquering foe.

"THE SEASON OF DEWS AND STARS."

BALLATA.

Thitherward by the crystal streams
  And cowslip meadows go ;
  Sweet shells will there breathe low
The music of the shining land of dreams.

Now golden Hesper sinks below the rim
  Of azure sky and now the fair young moon,
With silver glances piercing coverts dim,
  Makes dewy fields and shadowy ways to swoon
  With light ; and whiles the western wind's bassoon
Sounds in the tree-tops, eastward may behold
  The warrior Mars, on pathway trophy-strewn,
  His scarlet banner to the breeze unfold.

Thitherward by the crystal streams
  And cowslip meadows go ;
  Sweet shells will there breathe low
The music of the shining land of dreams.

INVOCATION TO SORROW—RONDEL.

Come, Sorrow, be my friend, and dwell with me ;
Thou hast been true when dearer ones denied,
When others failed, thou hast borne company,
  Henceforth as friend abide.

Tho' grim-visaged thou art, and solemn-eyed,
All the sweet uses of adversity
Thou hast taught, watching thro' the lone night-tide ;

The Beautiful, the Dear, by land or sea,
Are faithless gone and fleeting, far and wide ,
Thou, thou alone, thy pale face turned to me,
Keepst mournful guard beside.

GOLDEN CASTILE.

Oh land, Oh land, immortal, radiant realm,
Glimmering star-like where the billows rise,
Like Sirius or Algol, thro' mist and gloom
Thy glories fall upon our dazzled eyes.

Oh Paradise, thy winds have blown to us
Sweet savors of the violet and palm,
Of rose and orange, and all fragrant plants
That breathe upon the air their spicy balm.

And, sighing still, when stars gleam o'er the waves,—
Land of blest pilgrimage beyond the sea,
Bring us to thy calm shades and solitudes.
Land of soft rest and dreams, bring us to thee.

For there pale dawn brings not return of tears,
Nor shades of night regret for by-gone days;
Glad is the pomp of thy bright morns, and night
Sees stars pass gleaming down eternal ways:

And all thy homes are golden palaces,
Whose towers scale the bluest heavenly height,
For they are heaven-built and their high walls
With beryl, pearl and sardonyx are dight.

Oh land, Oh land, where shining spirits dwell,
　Thro' amber mists thine angel forms arise;
Adown the long blue vistas slanting bright,
　They come and go, they look down with sweet eyes.

How oft we've seen the tall waves mount the sky,
　Above the bloody sun, and heard the wind,
Blow fierce across the foam: and all our cry
　Was for the happy land—the bright, the kind.

Our dearest entered there—long, long ago;
　In tender dreams their last kisses we feel,
And still, their voices call across the seas—
　"Come join us in the bright land of the leal."

Why should we buffet more the driven surge?
　We are so weary, desolate and chill,
Oh. lead us where celestial music sounds—
　Beside thy fountains clear, Golden Castile.

LOVE SONG.

Oh my dove, my undefiled,
　My fair one of the gentle eyes,
Tell me whither dost thou stray,
　Tell me where thy covert lies?

All day thro' forest and thro' field,
.　Sorrowing have I sought thee,
All day thy tender tones have lured
.　My steps o'er mountain and o'er lea:

And now the stars are born again,
　And daisied meadows have grown dim,
My foot is weary and 1 seek,
　In vain for thee within the rim

Of purple left us by the sun;
　　Now, too, the darkening air is still,
And thy love-calls no longer woo,
　　The night-dew on my locks is chill;

Oh my dove, my well-beloved,
　　Say where thou fliest with the sun ?
All night my soul faints for thy love—
　　Oh bid the agony be done !

AN AUTUMN PETITION.

My darling, why dost thou delay return ?
　　The summer that hath been so gay, is o'er,
And in the burning bush the oriole's nest,
　　Deserted hangs, and by the reedy shore,
Of yon low lake the golden-rod's in bloom;
　　The silken thistle flies upon the breeze,
　　The flame of autumn flecks the forest trees,
Oh love, it hath been summer whilst thou stayed,
　　In distant lands and thy return delayed:

And now so long have I awaited thee,
　　So long, oh sweetest love, with wistful eyes,
Expectant turned on every flaming dawn,
　　That drove the Day-star from the Eastern skies,
So long hath twilight mocked me with vain hope,.
　　Alas, I have grown weary and my heart
Rejects with sorry plaint the watcher's part;
　　My love, the frost is on the fields, oh haste,
With thy dear presence cheer the wintry waste!

THE HILLS OF LYNN.

WE wandered down the Hills of Lynn,
  My love and I together:
Cicalas, chanting fine and thin,
  Made musical the heather;
Within the vale the lamps, like stars,
Shone in the dusk, and ruddy Mars
  On high his pennon floated:
O love, O love, a song-bird there
  Sang for us, silver-throated.

O pleasant are the Hills of Lynn,
  In summer greenly growing:
When stars the twilight ushers in
  The reapers from the mowing
Come whistling homeward thro' the glade,
And each one watches for the maid
  To him most dear and pleasing,
While down the lane the loaded wains
  Creak after, loudly wheezing.

The Hills of Lynn, to me so dear,
  How shall I tread them lonely?
My sweet love is not with me here,
  Yon moon marks one shape only,—
One shadow drawn across the grass,
Where once were two—dear love, alas,
  I'd fain be here laid sleeping;
For wandering down the Hills of Lynn,
  Alone, sets me aweeping.

3

The Hills of Lynn, O the Hills of Lynn,
  Where we used to walk together!
I wish me dead on the Hills of Lynn,
  At the end of the golden weather:
I wish me dead in a cold, cold shroud,
  Deep under the withered clover,
For since he has gone has come a cloud
  The golden hill-slopes over.

THE WOOD NYMPH.

I sat alone in the crimsoning wood,
  Alone in my heart's meditation;
Nor insect nor bird was anywhere heard,
  But the sunbeams in silent filtration
Glanced thro' the oak-trees' fluttering leaves,
  And winds sighed a slow salutation.

The opaline air breathed bright overhead;
  Below, the slow streamlet's miniature tide
With soft silver tones crept over the stones
  And rippling anon down the mossy hill-side,
Fell into a basin rimmed with ferns
  And spangled with daisies pied.

Afar on the height slept the lazy blue haze.
  To which had the sun given fringes of gold ;
So silent its rest on the hoary hill's crest,
  It seemed to have stolen from regions of old,
Where on the Nile's wrinkled bosom, in dreams,
  The yellow-leaved blossoms unfold.

Then, as I looked, lo the curtaining shade
  By fingers unseen was lightly withdrawn,
And there, half asleep in the cleft of the steep,
  Lay a spirit akin to the sylphs of the dawn,
Who dance to the music of Pandean pipes,
  On the dew-wet and shadowy lawn.

A spirit akin to the sylphs of the dawn!
  Oh, fair was her face as the Phidian stone;
Her long lustrous hair, loose, golden and fair,
  Over the snow of her shoulders was thrown,
And under her eye-lids' shadowy blue
  The soul of sweet Cupid saucily shone.

BALLATA.

TO A CAGED RED-BIRD, SINGING AT NIGHT.

Singing of birch and hazel shades,
  All the night long, poor prisoner ?
  How sweet, in the green prime o' the year,
To rove on scarlet wings thy native glades !

As turning on my pillow at midnight,
  I hear thy clear and silvery pipe, sweet bird,
Then dream I of the thatch where the rose blows bright,
  And pale new leaves, with silken rustle stirred,
  Makes answer to the brooklet's gurgling word;
Thro' their burnished emerald drips the filmy gold,
  And the breath of pines and dew-berry blossoms white
Fills the throbbing air with perfumes manifold.

Singing of birch and hazel shades,
  All the night long, poor prisoner ?
  How sweet, in the green prime o' the year,
To rove on scarlet wings thy native glades !

THE FLIGHT OF HOPE.

Now yonder where that diamond Star
  Betwixt the gold and sapphire rides,
White wings I saw, that flashed afar—
  'Twas Hope that clomb the swelling tides;
An hour ago her large een shone
  On me, now 'cross the midnight skies,
Hailing each seraph singer of the starry zone,
  She voyages toward Paradise.

A SONG OF THE SEA.

A song of a maid on the white sea-beach.
As far as ever the eye could reach
Were shifting billows and pale sea-foam :
(Fly, beautiful wings, Oh, fly thou home).

The sunlight danced on the sapphire sea,
The clouds blew up and the breeze sang free,
And over the leagues of pale sea-foam
The silver sea-gulls drifted home.

Silver sea-gulls and sapphire waves !
But far out yonder the storm sprite raves,
While o'er the billows and pale sea-foam
A fair ship's sailing blithely home.

Ye ho, Ye ho ! the sailors sang,
A white dove o'er the waves she sprang,
And under the billows the mermaids spread
Long yellow sea-weed for a bed.

Silver sea-gulls they dip and soar,
Sapphire billows sing round the shore,
And under the sea-foam lie the dead,
On the yellow sea-lichens outspread.

TRANSITORY—RONDEL.

Thy colors, rainbow, gainst the gray,
  Too soon they go, too soon they go ;
In track where flees the dying day
  Soon fades thy iridescent glow.

The young mid-summer moons that sow
  With gold the ripples of their way,
Too transient is their shining show.

But these, the angels of delay,
  Sweet passions that our fond hours know—
More dear, more brief, their tender sway—
  Too soon they go, too soon they go !

AT THE CATHEDRAL DOOR.

Sweet voices issue from the dark cathedral.
And sweet neath the arches the organ notes swelling,
Where penitents lowlily bow them in prayer :
    "O Lamb of God who taketh
      The sin of the world away,
        Have mercy on us."

Now over the tower hangs the moon's sickle—
Thin, silvery and dim, with one star companioned :
In the silent blue air leaves silkily flutter :
    "O Lamb of God who taketh
      The sin of the world away,
        Have mercy on us."

Since sunset, far have I journeyed thro' darkness,
And shadowy pathways, fragrant, dream-haunted:
Like the gateway to heaven the loved temple gleams:
  "O Lamb of God who taketh
    The sin of the world away,
      Have mercy on us."
    Give us thy peace."

TWILIGHT SILHOUETTES.

WHERE the shadowy gloaming softly steals
  Along the wind-blown willowy slopes,
A sound of mourning doves murmuring sad appeals;
  A sound of bells that chime and call
  From airy heights of ivied belfrys tall,
Where mounts the star on silver wheels.

Where swallows darkly rise and dip
  Across the rising moon's red shield,
A sound of honey-bees about the roses' lip;
  A sound of flutes from far away,
  Where dark against the gleaming verge of day,
The swallows nimbly soar and dip.

Where the shivering witch-elm gauntly throws
  Her weird shape on the wasted sward, .
A sound of crickets where the scarlet lily blows;
  A sound of fountains neath the leaves,
  A sound of whispering thro' the tawny sheaves,
Where the slim witch-tree's shadow grows.

OUT OF TUNE—Rondel.

I'm out of tune; the day goes drear,
  The skies are not of June,
There's neither sun, nor song, nor cheer,
  Because I'm out of tune.

Dead roses on dead grasses strewn,
  Gray clouds and blown leaves sere,
Wild winds that with rent boughs commune.

The grave, the winding sheet, the bier,
  The Judge's strict tribune,—
Thoughts of these bring nameless fear,
  When I am out of tune.

THE SHADOWS.

See the shadows, dark, fine-drawn and wavering;
So bird-like they hover, caressing the ground,
    Of nodding leaf and spray
    The images beautiful.

Here oft I walk sadly at evening,
The great stars watching with mystical eyes;
    And under my wandering feet
    The hovering shadows swing.

The wind sings a song in the oak-leaves,—
Sings sadly, methinks, of halcyons gone,
    And stars in their azure homes,
    Look down with mystical eyes.

The cricket chirps in the grasses;
Sweet rises the fragrance of hidden flowers.
    Unhappy, I wander and weep,
    With secret sorrow oppressed.

THE QUEEN'S MARIE.

Oh why did I grant thee this,
    The longed-for kiss ?
Oh why against thy breast
Suffer my cheek to rest ?
Did I think to shield from harm
It was that thy tender arm
    Drew me to thine embraces ?

If you know, yet you will not say;
    I had looked away,
Lest thy fondly passionate eyes
Should prevail o'er me, and thy sighs
Sweep from me my wavering pride,
Like sere leaves blown aside
    In mad euroclydons.

But again the old, old tale—
    When I saw thee pale
With stress of reproach and passion,
Then, vanquished in no new fashion,
I heeded thy oft-urged plea
And at last I granted thee
    These bitter-sweet reprisals.

THE WIND SPRITE.

Ah, friend, do you hear the windy blast
  Sobbing along the cold, dark fields ?
It drives before it, hard and fast,
  The thistle-top and fading leaf.

Áh, friend, do you mark the hollow cry
  In the chimney and round the eaves ?
It is like the wail of men who die
  Upon the deserted battlefield.

The stars with frost are faint and pale,
  The moon hangs low upon the hill;
The wraiths that wander, shivering,
  With cries the echoing forest fill.

The dead lie on the withered ground,
  With cold, white faces heavenward turned;
Pale are the wind-sprites gathered round
  To sing their mournful requiems.

The wind creeps through the bleak sand-bars;
  It finds among the willow trees,—
Stark, staring into the misty stars,—
  A drowned man in the blackened ooze.

He stares into the misty stars,
  Outstretched and cold upon the sedge;
The wind creeps thro' the bleaching bars
  And scatters leaves about his head.

Bethink you how the hill-side tombs
  Shine far athwart the cypress shades!
And there, in midnight's icy glooms,
  The sad wind wanders up and down:

It wanders among the pallid stones
  And lightly treads the glistening rime;
May'st hear what melancholy groans
  It utters o'er the unheeding dead.

Both near and far, in ghostly round,
  That spirit passes in the night,
And they that waken at the sound
  Shudder and seek companionship.

A warm hand in the darkness bleak,
  A touch of sweet humanity,
Or but a soft breath on the cheek,
  To cheer the unearthly loneliness.

TWAIN—THE DOUBLE STARS.

Sweetest sister, thou art fair
Smiling thro' thy gilded hair:
More than sister, sweetest heart,
We can never live apart!
Twain, in loyal union one,
Before the moon, beyond the sun—
Thus we sail the bubbling sea,
Forever joined in ecstasy.

O God of Destiny—whatever power
Is sovereign of man's brief, unhappy hour,
What gift have I desired of thee but death?
The stilled hand and heart, and lips whose breath

Is spent forevermore ? Only dumb peace,
Quiescent restfulness and sweet surcease
Of grief! Not glittering gold, nor glory, I,
Nor fame have sought, nor with the proud to vie,
But only this—a boon so small—to sleep
Among the shades, without a dream to creep
Into the close cells of the drowsy brain
And burst its crumbling filaments in twain.

THE CHORISTER.

Into the Chapel came my love
  To sing with the choir one holy day;
Each window there was a chrysolite,
  Tall angels marking the shining way
Where sunbeams thwarted the azure gloom;
  My love looked up, and in his eyes
Was the hue of violets dusk in bloom.
  He saw not me nor the angels tall,
Nor the fisherman walking upon the wave,
  But, crowned with halos, the blessed one,
Stretching His tender hands to save.

In the midst of the holy place I heard
  A sound of pipes played soft and low,
And the choir aloft in the golden gloom,
  Responded with voices sweet and slow;
Lilies and roses dreamed beneath.
  The roof was azure studded with stars,
And o'er the censer's fragrant wreath
  Was writ in gold a word of God.

He saw not me nor the angels tall,
  Nor any face of the waiting throng,
With eyes that dreamed on fairer heights,
  His soul ascended with his song.

And as he sang, it seemed to me
  I heard the heavenly choir draw near,
I heard the rustle of soft wings,
  I heard the harps and cymbals clear;
Oh, as he sang my sorrow ceased,
  And on my heart descended peace,
And like a prisoner released,
  It joyed once more in liberty.
Oh, sweet his voice, upsoaring light,
  Till in the vaulted arch it rang—
Methought 'twas seraphs' songs I heard,
  When with the choristers he sang.

But he sees not me nor the waiting throng,
  Nor the roses symbolizing love;
Neither dark nor fair, with dreamful eyes
  Beholds the form of a snowy dove,
With outspread wings 'gainst the violet shade,
  Hovering high in the air above.

THE ROSE.

THERE, royal blossom, golden rose,
Go, nestle in your last repose!
  Dim is this tiny grave you fill
  And very shallow, very still;

Go, take your rest—you've done your part,
You've brought his message, won my heart;
    Here, withered, pale and dead, you lie,
    Sweet rose of one fond memory:

This morn you lay against his breast—
Ah, happy rose, for such a rest!
    Then, looking down with eyes so blue,
    " A little gift I have for you,"
He said, and gave the rose to me:
And, now, I wonder did he see
    The kiss pressed on these petals fine
    And guess the passion in that sign ?

I wonder why my heart should ache ?
Do hearts, for careless friendship, break ?
    Indeed I merely meant to flirt,—
    Yet, somehow, somewhere, something's hurt!
Oh, golden rose, beneath the skies
Never saw I sweeter eyes,
    And, ah, what wealth would not I give,
    Only in their light to live!

L'ENVOY

There, be hidden, golden rose,
    Be buried in your silent tomb:
Heigho! before the moons of June,
    He will have plucked another bloom
And heard the nightingale's low tune
    A dozen times, while you and I
    In dust and darkness pine and sigh.

THE MOON-FLOWER.

THE light is flying; now the silver dew
Descends, and forth the moon peers from the blue;
  She sees the pale mists creeping thro' the vales
  Where willows ever whisper plaintive tales;
When all the world is shadowy and calm
And all the drowsy air is filled with balm,
  Then the moon-flower does its gleaming bell
  In leafy bowers display: Oh, wilt thou tell
What charm or spell or what unearthly power
Hath called thee to the magic of this hour?

The light is fading; now the silver dew
Descends and forth the moon peers from the blue;
  She sees mid shades below an answering face
  As fair as hers and curved in youthful grace;
Oh sweetly tell us, melancholy maid,
Why dream you sadly in the lonely shade?
  Methinks for hopeless love you pine and sigh,
Gazing so wistful from your window high,
And musing of the dear elusive bliss
That clings unto the sweetheart's greeting kiss.